W9-BXW-827

Celebrate Love Day!

Adapted by Alexandra Cassel Schwartz
Based on the screenplay "It's Love Day!"
written by Angela C. Santomero
Poses and layouts by Jason Fruchter

Simon Spotlight
An imprint of Simon & Schuster Children's Publishing Division • New York London Toronto Sydney New Delhi
1230 Avenue of the Americas, New York, New York 10020 • This Simon Spotlight edition December 2021
© 2021 The Fred Rogers Company. • All rights reserved, including the right of reproduction in whole or in part in any form.
SIMON SPOTLIGHT and colophon are registered trademarks of Simon & Schuster, Inc. For information about special
discounts for bulk purchases, please contact Simon & Schuster Special Sales at 1-866-506-1949 or
business@simonandschuster.com. • Manufactured in the United States of America 1021 LAK
1 2 3 4 5 6 7 8 9 10 • ISBN 978-1-5344-9594-4 • ISBN 978-1-5344-9595-1 (ebook)

It was a beautiful day in the neighborhood. "Happy Love Day!" Daniel Tiger said. "Love Day is the day when we say 'I love you' to the special people in our lives!"

"Good morning, Daniel," Mom Tiger said. "Ugga Mugga!"
Mom and Daniel rubbed their noses together. "Ugga Mugga"
was Mom's favorite way to say "I love you." And Daniel loved it too!

Margaret, Daniel's baby sister, was playing in the living room. "Happy Love Day, Margaret!" Daniel said.

Baby Margaret was still too young to say "I love you" with words. Instead, she gave Daniel a great big hug!

Daniel laughed and sang,

♪ ♫ *"Find your own way to say 'I love you!'"* ♪ ♪

Daniel had a grr-ific idea. He would make paper hearts to give to everyone at school. It would be his way of saying "I love you!" Daniel gathered construction paper, crayons, and glue.

First, Daniel cut out a heart and drew a picture of a pink tutu on it. "This card will be for Katerina!" Daniel said.

Then Daniel chose a piece of green paper. "I'll draw a tiny little book. It will be for O the Owl!" he said.

Making paper hearts was grr-ific!

Soon it was time to go to school. Daniel put all his paper hearts into a basket and headed outside.

"Hi, Trolley! I made something special for you," Daniel said. He stuck a paper heart on Trolley. Now Trolley was all ready for Love Day too!

When Daniel got to school, he went to put his backpack away. Then he noticed something inside his cubby. It was a card with his picture on it! "Wow!" he said. But Daniel didn't know who had given it to him.

Daniel walked over to Teacher Harriet and gave her a paper heart. "I made this just for you!" he said.

"How creative! Thank you, Daniel," Teacher Harriet said.

Then Daniel pulled out the card that he had found in his cubby. "Did you give this to me?" he asked.

Teacher Harriet shook her head. "No, it wasn't me," she said.

Next, Daniel walked over to Katerina. He reached inside his basket and pulled out the paper heart with a tutu.

"Meow, meow! It has a tutu on it because I like to dance!" Katerina said. "Thank you, Daniel!"

Daniel gave a paper heart to Miss Elaina too. "I drew a rocket on it, because I know you love outer space!" he said. Daniel's paper heart made Miss Elaina so happy. "It's boomer-ific!" she said.

Katerina and Miss Elaina had a surprise for Daniel too.

"Is it the special Love Day card I found in my cubby?" Daniel asked.

Katerina and Miss Elaina shook their heads. They had never seen the card before. But they did make a special Love Day show just for Daniel! They danced and sang about how much they loved having him as a friend.

After the show, Daniel joined Prince Wednesday at the table. "Did you give me a Love Day card?" he asked.

"No, I didn't," said Prince Wednesday. "But I did want to say 'I love you' . . . by giving you one of my special rocks!"

"Tigertastic!" Daniel said. "And here's a royally purple heart I made for you!"

Daniel had one more heart left in his basket. "This one's for you, O the Owl!" he said.

"Hoo, hoo!" O the Owl cheered. "It's a heart that looks like a little, tiny book!"

Daniel had fun giving out his paper hearts, but he still didn't know who had left him the secret card in his cubby.

"I didn't give you the card," O said. "But I know who did! He's someone you love . . . and he likes to sail . . . and he wears a sailor's hat!"

"Who could that be?" Daniel wondered aloud.

Suddenly, Daniel turned around and found Grandpere! He had come for a special visit.

"Is this card from you?" Daniel asked Grandpere.

"It is from me! I love you, my little grandtiger!" Grandpere said. He gave Daniel a big hug.

Daniel was so happy to celebrate Love Day with Grandpere. "And I'm happy I could celebrate with you too, neighbor!" Daniel said. "Happy Love Day! Ugga Mugga!"